*All children have
a strong desire to read
to themselves...*
and a sense of achievement when they can do so.
The **read it yourself** series has been devised to
satisfy their desire, and to give them that sense
of achievement. The series is graded for specific
reading ages, using simple vocabulary and
sentence structure, and the illustrations
complement the text so that the words and
pictures together form an integrated whole.

LADYBIRD BOOKS, INC.
Lewiston, Maine 04240 U.S.A.
© LADYBIRD BOOKS LTD MCMLXXVIII
Loughborough, Leicestershire, England

Printed in England

The Sly Fox and Red Hen

by Fran Hunia
illustrated by John Dyke

Ladybird Books

Here is Red Hen.

Red Hen has a home
in a tree.

This is Sly Fox.

He wants to eat
Red Hen.

Sly Fox
has a bag.

"I will go and look
for Red Hen,"
he says.

Sly Fox looks
for Red Hen.

Red Hen is in her home
up in the tree.

Red Hen comes down
for some water.

Sly Fox jumps up into the tree.

Red Hen comes home.

"Sly Fox is here,"
says Red Hen.
"I have to jump up."

Red Hen is up here.

Sly Fox can't jump
up to her.

Red Hen says,
"You can't come
up here, Sly Fox.
Go home."

Sly Fox says,
''I can't go up to you,
Red Hen.
You will have
to come down here.''

''No, I will not,''
says Red Hen.

''Yes, you will,''
says Sly Fox.

Sly Fox runs
around and around.

Red Hen looks
down at him.

Sly Fox runs
around and around.

Red Hen is dizzy.

Red Hen falls down, down, down.

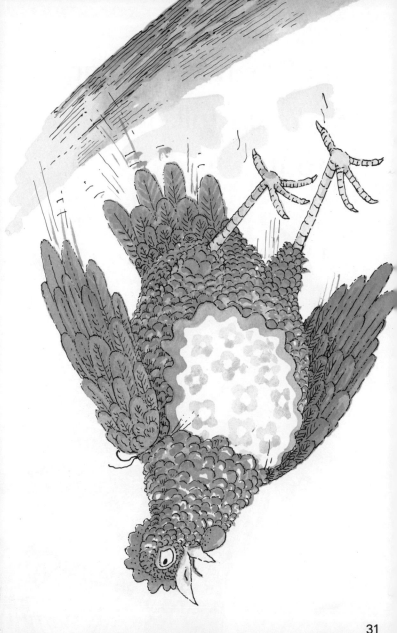

Sly Fox has the bag.
Red Hen falls
into it.

"I will go home
and eat Red Hen,"
says Sly Fox.
"Home we go."

34

Sly Fox runs
and runs.

It is hot.

Sly Fox wants
to sleep.

Sly Fox is asleep.

Red Hen gets out
of the bag.

Red Hen looks
for some stones.

She puts the stones
into the bag.

"This is fun,"
says Red Hen.

Red Hen runs home.

Sly Fox looks up.

He says,
"Red Hen is in the bag.
I will go home
and eat her."

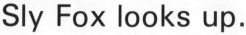

Sly Fox runs home.

He says,
"I will put Red Hen
into the hot water."

Red Hen is not
in the bag.

The stones are
in the bag.

They fall
into the water.

The hot water
splashes Sly Fox.

Red Hen likes
her home in the tree.

Sly Fox will not come
to look for her
any more.